The Spring Rabbit

An Easter Tale by Angela McAllister

Illustrated by Christopher Corr

Frances Lincoln
Children's Books

One winter morning,
a sunbeam slipped between the trees
and danced on the glistening snow.

Its warm touch stirred Spring from her long sleep.

As she woke up, winter melted around her.

Spring walked
through the woods.

Grass grew at her feet.

Her breath thawed icicles.

Leaves and blossom
appeared on the trees.

Whatever she touched
came to life at her fingertips.

Spring found a little bird, lying in the snow.

Gently, she picked him up. The bird was so cold and weak
that she could hardly hear his tiny heart beat.

"Don't give up, little one," she said.

"Winter will pass, now that I am here.
I shall make you warm and strong again."

Spring stroked the little bird.
She turned him into a rabbit, with thick, soft fur.

"Now you have a warm coat," she said.
"Follow me and there will be fresh grass to eat."

Rabbit looked
at his strange new paws.
He twitched his
whiskery nose.

The fresh grass smelled delicious,
so he tried it and it tasted good.

Spring walked on, across the meadow.
She woke the winter sleepers in their burrows and dens.
She made bright flowers bloom and called
newborn lambs out to play.

Rabbit hopped after her,
nibbling all he could eat along the way.

Before long, Rabbit felt warm and strong.
"How can I thank Spring for giving me this new life?" he wondered.
"I have nothing to give her in return."

He hadn't noticed that his friends,
the birds of the woods, had been watching.

That night they came to him:

the sparrow and the magpie,

the owl and the woodpecker,

the blackbird, the nightingale,
and the little wren.

Each one brought
an egg from its nest.

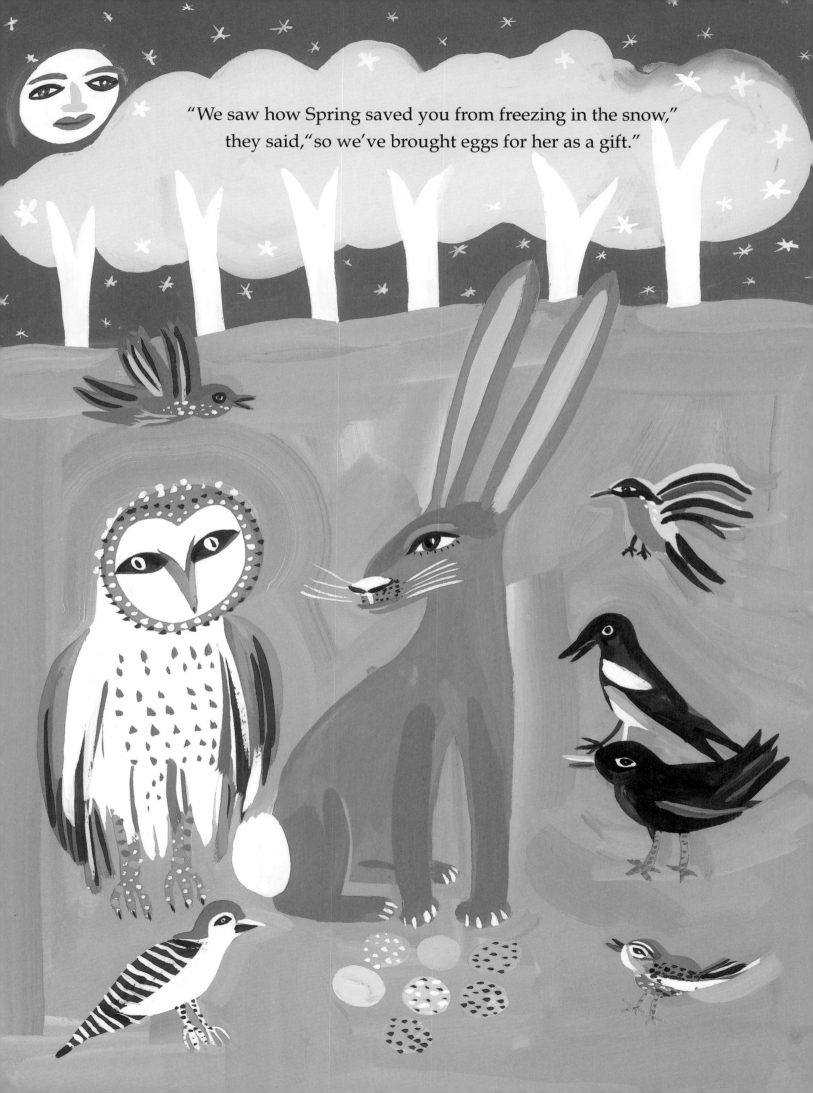

"We saw how Spring saved you from freezing in the snow,"
they said, "so we've brought eggs for her as a gift."

The next day, Rabbit thanked his kind friends.
"I shall make a basket to put the eggs in," he said.

When the basket was ready,
Rabbit wrapped the eggs in new leaves
and brightly colored petals, and laid them inside.

Spring was delighted with her present.
"It's a beautiful gift," she said.
"Thank you. But I cannot carry a basket.
My hands must be free
to make things grow."

Spring showed Rabbit a village nearby,
still deep in winter snow.

"Take the eggs to the
children there," she told him.
"They have been waiting
for me to arrive so
they can play in the
warm sunshine.

When they wake tomorrow and see these colorful eggs,
they will know that I am here."

Rabbit waited until the children went to sleep,
then he hopped across the moonlit snow to the village.

He found the children's winter hats, each one round
and cosy as a nest, and tucked the eggs inside.

When the children woke next morning they were surprised to find the eggs,
brightly decorated by the leaves and petals wrapped around them.

"These are the colors of Spring,"
they cried excitedly. "Winter must be gone!"

They looked out of
their windows.

The sun was shining, the snow had melted,
and a fresh, green world was
bursting with new life.

The children dressed quickly
and rushed outside to play.

Rabbit watched them splash in the stream,
skip with the lambs, and pick flowers for their hair.

Then all the birds of the leafy woods
sang together.

And Spring danced on, over the hill, chasing winter away,
with Rabbit hopping happily beside her.